A Suit
of Light

Also by Anne Hébert

FICTION
Am I Disturbing You?
Aurélien, Clara, Mademoiselle, and the English Lieutenant
Burden of Dreams
The First Garden
In the Shadow of the Wind
Kamouraska

POETRY
Day Has No Equal but the Night

A Suit
of Light

Anne
Hébert

A Novel
Translated by Sheila Fischman

Published in 2000 by
House of Anansi Press Limited
34 Lesmill Road, Toronto, ON M3B 2T6
Tel. (416) 445-3333
Fax (416) 445-5967
www.anansi.ca

First published in French as *Un Habit de lumière*
in 1999 by Éditions du Seuil

Distributed in Canada by
General Distribution Services Ltd.
325 Humber College Blvd., Etobicoke, ON, M9W 7C3
Tel. (416) 213-1919
Fax (416) 213-1917
E-mail cservice@genpub.com

04 03 02 01 00   1 2 3 4 5

Canadian Cataloguing in Publication Data

Hébert, Anne, 1916–2000
[Habit de lumière. English]
A suit of light

Translation of: Un habit de lumière
ISBN 0-88784-173-2

I. Title. II Title: Habit de lumière. English.

PS8515.E16H3313 2000   C843'.54   C00-930949-7
PQ3919.H37H3313 2000

Cover design: Angel Guerra
Page composition: Joseph Gisini/Andrew Smith Graphics Inc.
Cover photo: Leslie Derene/Photonica

THE CANADA COUNCIL   LE CONSEIL DES ARTS
FOR THE ARTS   DU CANADA
SINCE 1957   DEPUIS 1957

We acknowledge for their financial support of our publishing program the
Canada Council for the Arts, the Ontario Arts Council, and the Government of Canada
through the Book Publishing Industry Development Program (BPIDP).
This book was made possible in part through the Canada Council's translation grants program.

Printed and bound in Canada

A Suit
of Light

I

Rose-Alba Almevida

It's me that you see through the wide-open window of my lodge. On the street side. Me, leaning out the window for a breath of air. My head, my hair, my beloved face, my round shoulders, my heavy bosom, my pink satin dressing gown — all the most beautiful things that I possess, I show off through the window. I display the top part of myself, fully clothed, for the people walking by. Starting at noon, when I get up, and if the day is fine. As for the bottom part, it's still me, body and soul in satin, my well-rounded rump, my short legs, and my narrow feet. O the little mules that dangle from the tips of my toes, swaying like two flying birds. All of it carefully sheltered, hidden in the shadow of the kitchen behind me. I seem to be looking outside but, in reality, I am caring for my own person, in secret. I think about myself all the time. And about money. The money I need to become more and more myself, without blemish from top to bottom, bottom to top, all of me exposed to the bright sun of fame. My only son, Miguel, is with me, in the same unbearable dazzle of light. A real little torero in his suit of light. Whether he's naked or dressed my son shines and I, his mother, shine along with him. Olé! Olé! I hear the cries of the frenzied crowd. It's my son they acclaim. I inhale the blazing dust of the bullring. The furious gallop of the dying beast goes past my face. The smell of blood and death pursues me all the way to the foreign city where I am a concierge, at 102 rue Cochin in the fifth arrondissement of Paris, France.

Madame Guillou

Her name is Rose-Alba Almevida and she is taking the air at her window. Now, lightly, she moves her elbows on the window ledge. Tiny grains of dry black dust cling to her skin. She spits on her fingers and carefully cleans her elbows. She looks abstractedly onto the street. She sees her son who is drawing on the sidewalk with coloured chalk. This reassures her and allows her to return immediately to the very depths of herself, to the place where everything is dream and splendour. She's well aware that every-thing is happening in her head, but nothing in the world can stop her from daydreaming as she pleases, until a gnawing hatred for the life given to her sweeps over her like an equinoctial tide.

Rose-Alba Almevida

Rosa, Rosie, Rosita, Spanish rose, fiery and pungent, Rose-Alba Almevida, impulsive and supreme: I rhyme off the forms of your name, a superb litany. Let not a hair on your head move, nor your breath under your satin robe, let nothing reveal the soul you hide.

I plunge into silent furious longings for four-star hotels, for expensive cars with liveried chauffeurs, for luminous makeup, for unctuous creams, for indelible mascara, for vintage wines, for furs, especially for furs, red or silver fox, spotted panther, soft sable, so that I will be forever changed into a wild beast, fierce and splendid, made for love and consecration. These dreams come when I am mad on the inside and appear distracted on the outside.

Madame Guillou

Miguel Almevida. Seven years old. Huge eyes. White transparent skin that, when his clothing allows, reveals a tangle of blue veins. White shirt. Patent-leather shoes. Thin as a matchstick. Too delicate no doubt for the affronts of life.

Miguel Almevida

The sidewalk, grey as boredom. My coloured chalks go back and forth across the grey of boredom. Red, green, blue, yellow, white, violet. I place colour on the stagnant boredom of the sidewalk. The chalk screeches in my fingers, it crumbles and is crushed. I lay down straight lines. I draw the plans for my future house. Sick and tired of the crowded little lodge, of the toilet in the yard, of the faucet on the landing. French people, third-rate like all of them, go back and forth along my sidewalk. Shamelessly, their hurried steps erase my lines and colours. My mother would say that I ought to bite their toes very hard to punish them. That would teach them to respect other people's work. It's what she thinks when she has to scrub the staircase buried under layers of wax and dirty, muddy footprints that come from who knows where and sabotage her work step by step.

I have to pass the chalk over every half-obliterated line, brighten every colour that's been blurred, and then my drawing will be clear and precise and visible from one end of the street to the other. Here is my house, I dream it up as I go. A good twenty rooms, lined up along a corridor that's broad and deep as an avenue at the Place de l'Étoile. Small salon, medium salon, grand salon, small kitchen, medium kitchen, big kitchen, small dining room, medium dining room, big dining room, huge W.C., a second huge W.C., a third huge W.C., an immense bathroom, a very immense bathroom, an endless games room, and a very deep, wide, high, magnificent bedroom. Me, standing in the very middle of that wide, high, deep, magnificent bedroom. I am waiting for my husband and I proclaim it very loudly. Arms crossed, standing in the middle of the matrimonial chamber, I wait for him to arrive. My mother, who looks like an ancient mummy, sticks her head out of her wrappings and very angrily orders me to repeat that remark.

"I'm waiting for my husband!"

She yells so loudly the whole street can surely hear her: "You're sick in the head!" And she pulls the window shut.

My father is back and there are things going on between my mother and him behind the closed window, its drawn curtain. It's always that way as soon as the window or the door closes on them. I've been driven away, excluded, kicked out, and the two of them are inside whispering, arguing, laughing very loudly, and then moaning as if they were sick, my mother in particular, as if she's about to give birth. The silence that follows is like the end of the world. I feel like crying right there, all by myself, all dirty, covered from head to toe with the different colours of chalk, standing on the sidewalk, my feet planted in the middle of an imaginary bedroom. I must wash myself. To erase the sidewalk dust from my clothes and the traces of chalk from all over me. O my beautiful patent-leather shoes, what a disaster! They resemble my mother, they are ruined like her behind her window, and the water that she'll have to fetch in a bucket from the landing, her manner casual, her head high, and her dressing gown all wrinkled. In the middle of the day. A beautiful Sunday when my father looks dashing and has nothing to do. I know very well what they talk about before they collapse into moaning and the great deathly silence that follows. "Money! Money!" demands my mother. My father grunts and claims that she spends faster than he earns. Insults on both sides. Sometimes a few loud slaps on my mother's lovely behind. The cascade of her laughter.

I wait. I pace the sidewalk. I cool my heels. I wear out my wonderful shoes. I wait for the window to open again. One day I'll go away for good.

Three p.m. The window clatters open. The outside air rushes inside again. I follow the air into the house and I say, "I'm hungry." My father shuts the window. I have to sit at the table, my hands daubed with dust and chalk. There's not a drop of water in the house.

My mother doesn't yell at me to wash my hands. She's miles away, farther than ever, and all languid as a result. She has put on a blue dress and bracelets that clink on both arms. My father is puffing away on a Gauloise. His pride in smoking so powerfully and so deeply is equalled only by his dazzling smile between two puffs.

I eat surrounded by his smoke, I drink surrounded by his smoke, I breathe the smoke from after love. My dirty hands are in the shadow of the smoke. The silence around me is so great I can hear the smoke breathing its little mouse breath onto my face. I want to cry.

All at once the half-cold meal, the absence of conversation around the table, their stunned looks, and my own urge to cry — all were finished. Through the window barely open again, people could see that my father wasn't wearing a shirt. All the smoke went outside, swept away the personal stories of us, the Almevidas, evaporated in blue curls, this Sunday, September 25th.

My father's shirt is draped over the back of a chair, white as the Immaculate Conception in the churches, starched as the priest's surplice on Corpus Christi. A ray of sunlight has slipped under the chair. My father's pointed shiny shoes become illuminated beacons.

Pedro Almevida

In the time it takes Rosa to get ready, to put on all her frills and makeup, I'll have walked around the block two or three times. My son's hand in mine, my shiny shoes in front of me. The whiteness of my shirt matches that of my son's. Washed and changed at my insistence, now he is trotting along at my side. He insisted on wearing a mauve T-shirt with a green Mickey Mouse, but I was adamant and wouldn't yield. A man has to do what's right. Whiteness and polish on Sunday: that's as it should be. And memories of the corrida pop into my mind and armfuls of jasmine follow after.

If only I knew why my son's hand slips so quickly from my rough construction-worker's grip. The hand is too coarse and virile no doubt for a child who still wavers between girl and boy, whose mother dotes on him five days out of seven. In this foreign city the honour of Spain is assured by me, Pedro Almevida. My son Miguel shares that honour with me, he is bound to me, hand in hand, white shirt against white shirt, pointed shiny shoes — a double pair — walking at a good clip down boulevard Saint-Germain between four and five p.m. on this fine Sunday in September. Anticipation and impatience growing as I watch for the gorgeous embodiment of the fiesta herself, loosed upon the grey city, to appear at the corner of the street.

Miguel Almevida

Here she is! Here she is! She's wearing a miniskirt. You can see her big knees and, higher up, her fat thighs. The skirt stops there. A kind of little shirt cut from the same gold as her dress. I don't believe my father can love. He's too amazed to say a word. As for me, I get used to the idea of a tiny dress made of gold, an abbreviated sun that makes way for my mother's knees and thighs, gleaming and shining in their own way the length of the street.

My father says tonelessly: "We're going back to the house."

We followed my father home. But it was obvious that my mother thought the walk was too short when she'd taken so much trouble to get all dolled up. Her suppressed anger as great as my father's. Both pretended to walk along the sidewalk normally, their heads in the air as if they were trying to grab and harness the wrath of the storm clouds overhead, should the need arise.

They've quarrelled. Traded insults. Fought. Roaring like bulls in the ring. Rolling on the floor from one end of the tiny kitchen to the other. Breathing their dying breath. On the verge of a blackout or a fatal cramp.

After they had barely recovered, they took me out of the broom closet where they'd put me. They took stock of the battle's final toll. For my mother, a ruined dress, twisted bracelets, bruised arms and legs, a black eye. For my father, claw marks and tooth marks all over, and a broken rib. My mother weeps for her dress and her eye. My father promises to buy her another dress and a slice of steak for her eye. It's easy to see that he suffers a thousand deaths with every breath. My mother covers his chest with kisses, to glue the rib back together, she says. It's obvious that she is sincere and remorseful.

Rose-Alba Almevida

I'll buy the dress myself from a chic boutique on rue de Sèvres. The most beautiful and most expensive. The longest, too. He'll have nothing to object to as far as the length is concerned. As for the rest, he'll be dazzled. Except for the price, maybe. I'll think of something. That will teach him. I'll be as elegant as Diana was with Dodi Fayed, cruising on a yacht. My husband's head is sure to turn in the presence of such grace and beauty. To make love with him right then — as usual, when it strikes his fancy — I'll take off my new dress and carefully hang it up, safe from the tumults of love.

Miguel Almevida

Home from school earlier than usual and, silent as the air we breathe, saw everything without her seeing me. My mother took the vacation money. She closed the blue box and put it back with the dust bunnies under her bed. She left to pursue her own schemes and I stayed all alone in the deserted house with mine.

I dress and apply makeup carefully, as my mother always does before she steps outside. I take the dress that was ruined in the brawl and tossed in a heap behind a chair and slip it over my head as if it were a golden chasuble. Tubes and jars, brushes of all kinds, stiletto heels, and black tights make me look like some strange and slovenly girl. I have just enough time to rejoice at my weird image in the pitted mirror that hangs on the bedroom door when suddenly my mother is back, carrying a big box marked "Marie-Christine."

You can only be crazy about my mother's new dress. No queen, no movie star has anything like it. Velvet and sequins. No night riddled with stars is as black and glittering. Donkeyskin had better behave. My mother turns and spins at the mirror. I wait for her to see me in all my finery and marvel at me as I marvel at her. The two of us ecstatic at ourselves and at our doubles. Accomplices and sweethearts.

At last! She's seen me!

"Christ almighty! Am I dreaming? What if your father saw you!"

With no consideration for the golden dress or the black tights I put on my head to suggest a woman's long braids, she smacked my rear, and my high-heeled shoes fell off. She didn't hit too hard and I didn't cry. What's most important is that I still have hope in my heart that one day my mother will accept me as I am, outrageously made up, with purple nails, and long hair hanging down.

By sheer coincidence, my father decides that very night that I have to take karate lessons at the local school. One thing is certain, both my mother and I have secrets that must be kept from my father at all costs.

Rose-Alba Almevida

I hemstitch. All day long I hemstitch. The lady on the first floor complains about the heat. I hemstitch. The gentleman on the sixth floor is shivering. I hemstitch. Heat and shivers. They have their problems. I have mine. I won't touch the heat. I have hemstitching to do. I have no time to attend to the heating. The lady on the first floor is menopausal, the gentleman on the sixth is a nudist. What do they expect from me? I have hemstitching to do for Madame Guillou on the fourth floor. Piles of sheets and pillow-cases, thread pulled tight and knotted. Madame Guillou, who's very old-fashioned, is preparing a traditional wedding for her daughter. She'll have her trousseau, that overripe girl who is finally being married off. I hemstitch from morning till night. I stop dead and stow it all under the bed when my husband comes home in the evening. It's important that he not catch me sewing. I fear his questions. If he knew why I need money so badly he'd kill me. The blue box for our vacations under the bed — empty. He couldn't bear that and I would be dead in no time. Be brave, poor little me, this is just a difficult moment to get through. Day after day till the whole trousseau is ready. Afterwards I'll rest and I'll dye my hair Venetian blonde. My mind is made up.

Miguel Almevida

My mother is sewing furiously. I wonder what she's going to do with all those sheets. Maybe she'll open a four-star hotel. I'd love to roll around in sheets like those. It would be a change from the rags they make us wear for karate, for the exalted brutality of a deadly virile game. I fall to the floor so often I'm covered with bruises.

Yesterday my father took me to my karate lesson by force, dragging me by the arm the whole way.

There's been a leak in the cellar. My mother still pulls thread. People have been knocking at the door to her lodge for a good half-hour. My mother still does her hemstitching.

"Madame Almevida! Madame Almevida! The place is full of water! The cellar is flooded!"

"I'm coming! I'm coming!" my mother shouts, and she snaps a thread with her teeth before calling the plumber.

My God, this house is exhausting! People going in and out all the time. I don't know where I can go to live the life of a well-behaved child: learning my lessons, doing my homework, examining the bruises all over my body, and cursing my father in peace.

Rose-Alba Almevida

I pleaded, wept, threatened, simpered, and fondled endlessly. To go dancing at a club. To wear my dress from Marie-Christine for the first time. My husband grumbled, yelled, mentioned once again how hard it is to earn money and how easy it is to spend. But when he saw me in my black velvet dress riddled with glittering stars, standing erect in the middle of the kitchen, at the very heart of this rat's nest where the three of us live with no toilet or running water, he said, "Yes." He could only say "Yes" because he didn't suspect the price of the dress or its consequences for our vacation in Spain.

In exchange for all that hemstitching so skilfully pulled and knotted and already dearly paid for, Madame Guillou will look after Miguel until morning. I have the whole night ahead of me for dancing with my husband.

I love dancing, my whole body thrashing about rhythmically, my husband facing me, agitated and glorious. The two of us in the same wild and joyous whirl. Now and then an urge comes over me to try and dance close with someone else, to see if it would have the same effect as with Pedro Almevida, my husband.

As the night draws to an end, as the glimmers of light become ever softer and the cigarette smoke thicker, the slow number rocks the barely standing but warmly locked dancers like a population of the drowned swayed by a rising tide.

I'm drunk, more than from any drink, ready to bed any man who would hold me tightly against him while swords of fire pierced my body through and through. I close my eyes and I melt. My husband gives a hollow laugh and whispers in my ear to wait till we're home to pass out completely. I open one eye a bit and, over Pedro Almevida's shoulder, spy a broad grin without a face, nothing but the smile of an unknown man addressing me quite openly. My husband drags me outside as I cling to his arm and try to erase from my mind the unknown and beautiful strong white teeth that secretly devour me.

Miguel Almevida

It may be a rat hole but it's mine. I'm attached to it. I've been here since my mother left the clinic with a little bundle, me, in her arms. Three days after my birth. That was ages ago. And now they're chasing me out of my home so they can go to a club and live it up like teenagers. It's not the first time, either. Yet whenever they do it I'm scandalized in the same way. My own parents. To ship me off to Madame Guillou's on the pretext of inaugurating my mother's new dress. Under the coloured spotlights and strobe lights. At their age it's absolutely uncalled for.

Madame Guillou's black horsehair sofa dominates her living room. It's like an enormous sea creature glistening with water. Madame Guillou puts a hemstitched sheet on the sofa and gives me a red-and-white striped blanket that smells of mothballs. Horsehair is spiteful. It's hard and prickly. Slippery. I fall, I land on the floor. Twice. Hard enough to make new bruises. It's like everything else: I have to get used to it.

Morning. Foamy chocolate and hot croissants delight me more than I can say. I'm still overcome with happiness, the chocolate and croissants barely downed, in a state of deep contentment, when I realize that Madame Guillou's wrinkled face is really very kind. I kiss her flabby cheek.

Before leaving I spend a long time gazing at an adorable doll in a pretty dress that's sitting on a shelf. Behind my back Madame Guillou looks at me looking at the doll, her attention equal to mine, intense and indiscreet.

"That doll belonged to my daughter when she was a child. My daughter never liked dolls."

As I make my way home, slowly, dragging my feet down each step, I have all the time in the world to think that if life were arranged better, it wouldn't be wrong for Madame Guillou's daughter not to like dolls or for me to love them.

Pedro Almevida

I am the father, the husband, the *paterfamilias*. I have a thick black moustache that's carefully waxed and tapered at both ends, a carnivore's teeth, and a quick temper. Construction worker. Créteil, Nanterre, Villetanneuse, sometimes in the provinces too. My wife, Rose-Alba Almevida, is a concierge on rue Cochin in the fifth arrondissement. When I've made my fortune I'll go back to my native land. Ten or fifteen years of exile, if I have to. I'll exhaust my legal status as a foreigner in this foreign city. And go back home. I'll have a spacious house made of whitewashed adobe. Inside, every modern convenience. A small field beside it, planted with vines, as straight as a die. The ideal would be to spend nothing here. Except for what's necessary. Put everything aside. And go back to Spain. But now Rose-Alba Almevida, my wife, my spendthrift, my glory and my torment, lets my money slip away, fleet as mercury. It's true that I attain seventh heaven with her, both day and night. That's worth a little present now and then. As if I could afford it.

Miguel, Miguel, my son, look me in the eye once, only once, look me in the eye and I'll give you the earth.

I bought him a soccer ball in exchange for the doll I broke. He wouldn't take the ball and he hasn't stopped crying.

Maybe I was wrong to have wanted a boy so badly when Rosita was pregnant. It didn't bring me much luck. Before the ultrasound, I even told her quite seriously as she looked at me with outrage: "If it's a girl I'll throw her to the pigs."

Her grave and quivering voice: "If you ever do such a thing, Pedro my husband, I'll kill you."

Rose-Alba Almevida

"Madame Almevida! Madame Almevida! The garbage stinks in the courtyard! It's been three days now! Get rid of it, woman, and fast!"

Rosa, Rosie, Rosita, little feet, fleshy lips, round shoulders, the most beautiful woman to dance with, people are calling to you from the depths of hell, they want to see you on a dung heap, on a pile of rotting things, with your cool hands, your perfumed breath, your light heart. Use your dainty fingers to sew fine fabrics. Clandestine work, clandestine machinery, in aid of the vultures of the Sentier. Money! Money! I need money! I'm being robbed! Exploited like a blind negress. Money. Fast, before my husband checks the cash in the blue box under the bed. It could happen though that I'll hang myself first, like a charm at the head of the bed, swaying and sticking out its tongue.

"Madame Almevida!"

They say "Madame" to my face. But under their breath they call me "Marquise." I know they do. I know everything. Oh, if I could I'd empty their garbage onto their heads, but that's not in my contract, and I must fulfill its every clause to the letter. Under threat of being fired. So I'll dump the trash into those big containers, with orange or green lids, that you see on city sidewalks in the morning. But I'll put them out around midnight so I can sleep peacefully during the fine hours of dawn, as I like to do, with the grey shadows holding the chirping of birds as they answer one another from tree to tree.

After Operation Trash I'll take my son to bathe at the Bains des Patriarches, at Censier-Daubenton, where the towels are so big, the water so hot, and the tubs so deep.

My husband is in Saint-Nazaire nailing boards and putting up house frames. I'll be sleeping alone. I'll take the boy into my bed. The two of us in the sweetness that follows a bath. Poor little angel, he cried so hard when his father broke the doll Madame Guillou had given him.

Miguel Almevida

He did it on purpose. He picked her up by the feet and threw her onto the kitchen floor. My poor doll broken into a hundred pieces. Shattered. An old-fashioned doll, very brittle and gorgeous. He was all red, like the flag you wave before a bull to excite him. He's a bull himself, my father, breathing hard in his rage. He said again and again, as if he were cracked in the head: "No you don't, little boy! No you don't! Never!" And went out, slamming the door.

I cried so hard I could have drowned in my tears. A lake at my feet with pieces of doll floating in it, like crumbs on a plate for the birds. And now I've taken his place in the big bed, next to my mother. Too much happiness. Too much. Both of us, my mother and I, smelling good, warm and smooth in the same way after our bath at the Patriarches, close to one another now in the clean sheets. Twins in a single white shell. Yet I'm crying as if I were all alone in my folding bed on the floor of the kitchen, between the table and the buffet.

I finally fall asleep with my mother's feet against mine, "To warm me with your little furnaces," she said.

He came home sooner than expected and carried me, fast asleep, out of the big bed, like a sack of potatoes transported cautiously.

It wasn't till the next morning, as I was getting ready to leave for school, that I started gathering up my things.

Once I was there I told my plan to my friend Karine, who always listens to me and sometimes lends me her Barbie doll. "I'm leaving. My mind's made up. I'm not staying in the house with that stranger."

Karine asked me what stranger I was talking about. I told her it was my father.

Rose-Alba Almevida

That child is going to drive me crazy. My most expensive blush! My finest tweezers! My thickest eyebrow pencil! He took it all away with him in the red suitcase. He did it, he did it, my son Miguel who ran away this morning. It's now five p.m. And I, his mother, am going stark raving mad. My knees are quivering. My hands are freezing. Me, crazy, all by myself in the house. My husband in Saint-Nazaire. My son miles away. What bad luck! I'm suffering like a martyr in the olden days, in the convents of Spain. The police! Should I call the police? To hunt for my son like a criminal. My hair is too black, not yet dyed Venetian blond, I'll pull it out, one hair at a time, as a sign of despair.

For a good fifteen minutes now someone has been pounding on the door of the lodge. Madame Guillou is calling to me as if she were mad.

I'm coming, I'm coming, Guillou, Guillou, you asked for it. I'm foaming with rage and if I open the door to you, you'll see what it means to be a Spanish woman in *la furia* of living.

Miguel Almevida

I roamed the streets. All day long. Dragging the red suitcase. Changing arms. Setting it down on the sidewalk here and there, to rest. I was hungry. I was thirsty. I was afraid. I was cold. I cried a little. Night comes early in November. I felt the dampness of the night on my back. The city was at its worst. Malevolent and foul. The breath of the city on my neck. Hooligans breathing very close to me, their rotten eyes staring at me as I walked by. I decided to take refuge with Madame Guillou. Right away she took my hand and delivered me back to my mother. I didn't put up a fight, I was limp and contrite. Crying my eyes out. My mother held me in her arms, tightly enough to break my bones. I wailed in a voice so piercing that Madame Guillou stood there petrified, stabbed by my howls as if by a hundred Andalusian daggers plunged into her widow's heart.

Another night without my father. An entire night in my mother's bed. Myself all icy up against her, she blazing hot and musky after all the emotions I'd subjected her to while I was a runaway.

At dawn, my mother, who usually doesn't get up till noon, started shaking me the way she shakes her bedside rug from the kitchen window once a month, in a cloud of dust, fine grey incense swirling all the way up to the sixth floor. I thought I'd die from that shaking.

She said again: "No, no, I won't tell your father, I promised, but you do it again and I'll make mincemeat out of you."

I left for school without breakfast, my whole body trembling.

Pedro Almevida

I am the husband, the father, the master of the house. I put food on the table for my family. With my pay in my pocket, I go home. Here I am in the train. Ten days in Saint-Nazaire, hammering and nailing in the November wind and rain. I could take my wife right on the doorstep, the minute I arrive, I want her so badly. But first I want to make myself handsome, blazingly handsome, from head to toe. I'll put up with the filthy toilets at the train station for the time that it takes to shave and shower. I'll put on a clean shirt and the shiny shoes that go with it. I'll show up at the door of my house like a knight home from battle.

With every trace of sweat and toil erased, I go home. I close my eyes and already my arms are filled with her, my beauty, Rosa, Rosie, Rosita Almevida, my wife.

Rose-Alba Almevida

I'll have a surprise for him. I'll dye my hair. After a ten-day absence
he'll have a surprise. Myself, transformed. Into a Venetian blonde.
Claudia Schiffer, but better. More flesh on the bones. A golden
splendour emerging from the shadows like a blinding sun too long
held captive.

The hairdresser studies me, looks me up and down. For him I
don't exist. I'm just a head. No body or soul, just a head at the tip
of a lance for him to take and transform to his liking.

He talks as if he were dreaming out loud. He appears to see
what he's saying, clearly before him. It's obvious that I inspire him.
"I'll dye your hair. I'll cut your hair. I'll transform you drastically.
Let me do it, you're too dark, you have the beginnings of a moustache. I'll release you from the darkness. Leave, leave your
decapitated head in my hands. I'll make it into a resplendent idol."

What he says, he does. I am delivered into his hands like a dead
animal that's turned over and over, washed and embalmed. Once
the operation is over, there appears in the mirror before me a
golden sparkling creature who claims to be me. I behave myself
and dare not contradict her. Absorbed in my infinite contemplation.

"That's 600 francs," says the hairdresser.

I haggle with him. By way of payment I offer him the long hair he's cut off. He studies the heavy sheaf of black hair that has fallen to the floor. Gathers it up, holds it in his hands, hefts it, sniffs it. He maintains that it's Asian hair, straight and coarse, and that it's worthless next to a fine and silky Scandinavian mane. I offer to leave a deposit and come back tomorrow with the rest. The hairdresser smiles, shakes his head, says again softly, tenderly almost, like a cooing pigeon: "Cash, cash, cash, my lovely."

I offer him my gold wedding ring and take back the mass of my hair and cram it into my shopping bag. He accepts my ring after he's felt its weight and clinked it on the counter.

I go home, a tiny white line like an old scar on the fourth finger of my left hand.

Miguel Almevida

What I saw, what I heard between my father and my mother was
so frightening, I'll never be able to speak it without dying a second time. The first time, I was hiding under the kitchen table, my
jacket over my face, my fists over my ears. Waiting for catastrophe.
There won't be a second time, I swear. I couldn't bear it. Yet
images, words swirl around me still while I sleep.

"Get out, you aren't my wife any more. I don't recognize you."

A small blond head rises and bristles. "I'm someone else, blond
and desirable, a genuine star. Take me and you'll see how beautiful I am."

"What have you done with the long black hair that I loved?"

"Here, take it. It's yours."

She opens her shopping bag and pitches a black mop at his
head; he flings it to the floor and stomps on it.

My heart is beating hard enough to crack my ribs. I implore
the angels of the night. To come and pull a crimson curtain
over the high drama of family scenes. So I can curl up between
the sheets.

A little tune, light and persistent, slowly moves away with the
dream that's nearly over.

"The ring, the ring you gave me, Pedro my husband, I've lost it, I lost it on my way to the market."

Their voices, unrecognizable, singsongy, die somewhere inside me.

Pedro Almevida

She's lying. I'm sure that she's lying. I'll rub her nose in her lie. Oh,
she'll admit the truth in the end. There is female deception beneath
it. Sly dishonour to a man. It's not clean. It's diabolical like the Trinity,
the Incarnation, and everything else we don't understand. One day it
will be crystal clear. Everyone crowded into the Valley of Jehosha-
phat. The Last Judgment. The mysteries revealed. It's then that I'll
know for certain what my wife did with the gold ring given to her by
me and blessed by a priest in a church in Seville on May 28th, 1977.

I take her to the market at the hour when they hose down the
square. She and I bend over, looking down at the ground. Among
the puddles, the gleaming asphalt, lettuce cores, gutted oranges,
apple peels, overripe pears, all rotten things, swept away by the
gushing water. Gold ring, little wedding ring, are you here? We
might as well be trying to find a needle in a haystack. Rose-Alba
Almevida cries and says that it's pointless to look. She asks me to
forgive her. For nothing, she says. To do as I want, she maintains.
I'll kill her one day.

She is wearing tight black satin trousers and a bright orange shirt
with puffed sleeves. With her makeup on, something like shiny

little beads drop onto her cheeks from her eyelids. A marvel. I won't tell her that her legs are too short. I feel like being kind to her again.

She takes me to Madame Guillou's. Madame Guillou's bathroom. Tile on the walls and floor. Gleaming, blue and white. I'm here to fix the leaking radiator. Rose-Alba Almevida, my wife and my torment, feasts her eyes on the splendour of Madame Guillou's bathroom. I touch her arm to wrench her from her daze. Tears fill her eyes and her lips quiver like a child trying not to cry. When she's back in the lodge she says again and again: "It isn't fair. It isn't fair."

And she goes to the landing to get water from the faucet there.

I promise her that one day we'll have saved enough for her to have her own bathroom, white and blue. It will be in Spain, surrounded by vines.

She says that what she wants is a fur coat.

Miguel Almevida

The life that we have to put up with, day after day, ever since the construction site in Saint-Nazaire was shut down for good two weeks ago. My father is at home from morning to night, from night to morning. He smokes cigarettes one after another. When I go outside I can smell the smoke on me as if I were my father himself. I'm like someone walking around with a hundred lit cigarettes in his mouth. I reek of them. I'm only ten years old but it upsets me. I have to step over banks of smoke as soon as I'm inside my house. He is there watching me through the blue puffs of smoke. This is not the time to contradict him. It's as if he's watching a bull being released into the ring. I tiptoe past him. Above all he mustn't know that I skip rope at recess like a girl even though he's forbidden it.

At night I have a dream while he sleeps next to my mother, like a newborn gorged with cigarettes.

A skipping rope hangs down from the ceiling where it meets the wall. It unfurls downwards by itself, very slowly, like a snake descending. I know they're going to beat me with that rope, that's why it's coming towards me. I lie on the ground. I prepare myself for the beating. I beg my father: "Please, not too hard, I'm so tired."

Is it only in my dream that I cry out? The two of them come to my bedside, barefoot and in their nightclothes. They advise me to be good and to sleep the way the angels sleep, without a sound.

The end of a dark childhood on rue Cochin.

II

Jean-Ephrem de la Tour

Tall stature, small heart, black skin, white smile, green and blue feathers on top of my shaved head, I am Jean-Ephrem de la Tour. Dancer at the Paradis Perdu. Lights pointed all over my skin, from top to bottom, night after night. I'm turning into an American star. Silver wings fastened to my shoulders. I flame and I die in a single breath. I rule over a population of dancers and acrobats. While jugglers and snake charmers in the backstage shadows secretly indulge in base jealousies and the audience rises to its feet, giving me a thunderous ovation.

I meet him around five in the evening on my way to the post office. He, lost child, little heap of dejection, collapsed on a step of a staircase on rue Saint-Victor. I bend over him. "Hey, little beast! Better straighten up or you'll be hunchbacked. Unfold yourself, little beast, before it's too late."

Frozen with dread, he looks at me unblinkingly. Fear, unalloyed, in his wide-open eyes. I relish it. Will never forget this first fear in his eyes. Bound to him, the frightened child, by the terror that is visible all over his little person curled on a staircase on rue Saint-Victor around five p.m. Such is his destiny, no doubt, to be frightened by me. Such is my own, no doubt, to put the finishing touch on a dread already old, as if it were the original terror, within him. I tell him again to straighten up, not to stay there sitting on the ground. He obeys me as though he can't do otherwise. Fear trembles between his very long lashes. I give him a smile that shows all my inordinately white, strong teeth. I bow to him. I wish him a good day. I wish him a good evening. Ask him not to be afraid of me. Tell him that I'm good when I want to be and that I love him madly, just like that, at first sight, the way we love the sun when we rise in the morning. He says it's not possible and that his mother is expecting him for dinner. He wants to leave. I take his hand. I put his two soft blazing hands in my own hard one. I talk to him about the Paradis Perdu. I tell him about the dancers and acrobats, the music and chatter, the feathers and sequins, the barely pubescent boys and girls transformed under the footlights, carried away till dawn by their passion for life. He listens to me closely and dread works all its tricks in him and on him, skin-deep, like a fever that's subsiding. Seduction has its way and he asks me where to find the Paradis Perdu. I put a pass in his hand. Tell him I'll be expecting him tonight, backstage, and that he'll be able to see the whole show.

"See you later, little beast. Make sure that you're there."

He goes off so quickly, so agile and light, like a squirrel, that I wonder if he will still exist after this first meeting between us on rue Saint-Victor.

His name is Miguel Almevida. He whispered it in my ear before he disappeared like a vision of him that I might have had before dying.

I don't know yet that he has just turned fifteen.

46

Miguel Almevida

I've waited so long for this night filled with risk, without knowing I was waiting for it, timidly, amid the erosion of childhood, day
after day, despondent, often crying. And now the feast for which I
was destined, for all eternity, throbs softly like a quivering heart
behind the walls of the Paradis Perdu. Slipped through the darkness
of the streets for the first time, alone and dressed in my finery in the
night. Far away is my father, who's unemployed most of the time,
hidden by his smoke like a cuttlefish by its ink. Far away, too, is my
seamstress mother with her deafening sewing machine. The thieves
of the Sentier who exploit workers will have gotten off lightly. One
day my mother will be queen and I'll be the king at her side.

Tonight I make my entrance into the world. The world is opening before me. A little longer and I'll know the secrets of the earth.
Dear God, how innocent I am and how my knees are trembling.
This is the little hidden gate I must pass through to experience the
living splendour of the universe.

He is there behind the door, waiting for me as promised. Half-
naked, black, smooth, the eyes enlarged with kohl, the mouth
blood-red, the teeth awe-inspiring, green and blue egret feathers
on his head, silver wings on his shoulder blades, he is the angel of

darkness, born for his own ruination and for mine. His shadow on the wall is that of a giant, bristling with strange frills and flounces.

He tells me to go away and I go. He tells me come here and I come. Upon my obedience my happiness depends. When the curtain goes up on the show, I shall be ready to see everything, to hear everything. The very wellspring of the earth will be revealed to me then, in bursts of music.

He asks for something to drink and I fetch it, wandering the unfamiliar corridors and stairways where half-dressed boys and girls go back and forth, not yet ready for the show, in the process of being transformed into angels or devils.

He says again, Little Beast, do this, do that.

I murmur so quietly he has to bend over to hear me: "My name is Miguel Almevida and I'm not a beast."

He laughs so hard that his wings clash together on his back. He claims that it's a compliment, that for him the word "beast" is sacred and that only gods are entitled to be called it. In a deep voice, almost too deep, he adds: "Little Beast is fine, it's beautiful, it resembles you. Call me Beautiful Beast in return. And everything will be equal between us, the animal and the sacred. Except that I'm the one who is master."

He laughs again. His wings stir. He grabs my hand, places it against his naked chest. "Can you feel my heart beating, Little Beast? Stroke my heart, the way you'd stroke the breast of a black horse to reassure it before a race. In a few minutes I'll be on the track, pawing the ground and scared to death. Call me Beautiful Beast and wish me luck. Say break a leg, break a leg, break a leg, in my ear. Tonight the corrida will be terrible, I can sense it. They might cut off my ears and my tail as they do in your country. You'll no doubt be given the honours of the ears and tail. They'll bring them to you on a silver platter. Little Beast, idiotic and sweet, you'll know this very night what a real feast is. All of life, all of death, on a silver platter like the bloody head of John the Baptist.

He talks like a book that I've never read. He chokes with laughter. He straightens his wings. I stand there frozen, my hand on the naked chest that becomes misty little by little from a slight sweatiness like dew.

This man possesses the knowledge of good and evil, that's certain.

Three muffled knocks ring out in the dark. Everyone on stage. The feathers, the plumes, the fake jewels, the sequins suddenly appear, jostle me along the way, warm bodies brush against me, the mingled odours of girls and boys prickle my nose, go to my head. The black sun of nocturnal feasts will rise once again above the stage of the Paradis Perdu.

Between the dressing rooms and the stage I listen to the unleashed music, to the dancers' rhythmic feet. Noisy inhalations, laboured breathing dart across my face like quick drafts of air.

After this I'll never be the same, dressed in childhood as in a piece of clothing that's too tight.

The tallest and the handsomest of them all is Jean-Ephrem de la Tour. His long legs, his long arms, his misty chest, the whole of his body that rushes forward and soars, undulates and sways, contorts itself and comes undone, then immediately re-forms itself again, intact and pure, to the sound of some discordant music.

He wraps himself in a big towel and sweats so much it's as if he'd fallen into the Seine. Half-naked boys and girls bring him food and drink. He signals me to leave. "Get lost, Little Beast! I'm tired."

I go home, alone in the night as it draws to a close.

Rose-Alba Almevida

I no longer have a son. I disown him. I mourn him. I hate him. I could tear his eyes out. He came in at dawn, haggard, with circles under his eyes, exhausted as a hooker at daybreak. My husband says that's just fine, his son is now a man and it reassures him to know it. "Involved with a woman at fifteen," he repeats proudly. He laughs. While I cry. Probably Karine, the pale little freckle-faced nitwit who came here from the cold countries. What a disaster! Pedro my husband tells me to be quiet and let his son rest till late tomorrow morning. I obey and I fall asleep in the warmth of my tears.

Pedro Almevida

I have just one son who has never been mine. Hardly out of childhood and now he sleeps like a new man after love. Everything is finished between us without ever having begun. I am not the father. He is not the son. He's asleep now. In his dreams he is arming himself against me. He must grow and I must be diminished. So it is written.

I set my mind at rest. For a moment I remind myself of my inalienable rights as head of the household. I dictate my last wishes: a tough virile son finally out of school, which only numbs the mind, dropped into the world of work with nerves of steel and arms of iron. Let his strength have no equal but mine until I die. Amen.

Two men in a house is too many. Who will be the first to drive the other out?

Miguel Almevida

Night poured down over the city by the bucketful, laden with stars or with storms, night keeping watch around the streetlamps, encircling them, night, supreme, spilled out all around, outside, inside, even in the concierge's lodge on rue Cochin at the family dinner hour.

Patience, my soul. Another mouthful or two, another word or two exchanged around the table and the lights of the Paradis Perdu will be turned on like a beacon in the city and I will be free to run towards its strange forms of bliss. I drop my napkin onto the table. In anticipation my heart fills with spells and dread. I slam the door. I'm outside.

"That child is intolerable," says my mother.

"The girl who's got hold of him is a devil, that's certain," says my father.

"Sure, sure, sure. I have to know," says my mother. She gets up from the table, dons her red hunting jacket, her bright earrings, she goes onto the street, follows me from a distance all the way to the Paradis Perdu, buys her ticket, and sits in the front row, between two elderly gentlemen who ogle her greedily.

I don't notice my mother there in the dark until my gaze, shifting from the wings to the audience, settles on her by chance.

She came backstage after the show. They asked if she was there for an audition. A bunch of girls and boys, their makeup half-removed. They measured her, weighed her. Laughed at her. Cried, "Oh!" Cried, "Ah!" While studying the numbers on the ruler and the scale. They told her she was outside the norm, buxom and squat, she repeats "buxom" and "squat," mulling over the unfamiliar words as if they were insults. She weeps with rage.

Jean-Ephrem de la Tour approaches her, wrapped in his big towel. With one movement of his long upraised arm he waves away the mockers surrounding my mother. The towel is half-off him and she can see his black streaming chest. She looks and doesn't blink. He takes my mother's face very gently in his two hands, their orange palms, in the way one might hold a newly opened peony about to shed its petals.

"What a lovely face you have there, Madame!"

I cry out: "But she's my mother!"

He doubles up with laughter. The towel at his feet. He is immersed in his sweat and his laughter, almost naked before her. To her, he represents everything about the Paradis Perdu, its wonders and its infernal rhythms, the entire world of magic she's always dreamed about. My mother's desire to lose herself in the whirlwind is as strong as my own.

He asks for the towel which has fallen to the floor. He shivers and trembles. Says that he's going to catch his death of cold.

My mother's eyes are glued to me as I pick up the towel and drape it over the shoulders of Jean-Ephrem de la Tour in a way that lets my mother know I belong to this man, body and soul.

As I wrap him in the towel and rub him down vigorously, we exist so powerfully together, he and I, that it makes my mother want to fight me. Her dearest wish would be to be in my place, close to Jean-Ephrem de la Tour.

She declares that she's never seen anything as wonderful as the show at the Paradis Perdu. Then she says nothing for a long time, consumed by bitter silence.

Jean-Ephrem de la Tour steps into the shower. He exclaims: "Screw off, Little Beast, and take your mother too, I need to get some rest."

Rose-Alba Almevida leads me away, drags me by the hand as if punishing a child. On rue Cochin not even a small lamp is lit, the lodge is dark, more of a rat hole than ever. My father is no longer there.

Pedro Almevida

Out of my home, thrown onto the street, I'm outside my house like a snail without its shell. At the corner café I drink white wine. I search in vain for what's true and what's not. Try to untangle reality from dream. Sourness in me as if I'd eaten sour cabbage. I struggle to sort out my ideas. I kick the bar. Head down. I examine the fake marble. I see in it vague lines like the ones in my head. Determined to shake off all my concerns like dead leaves in autumn, I drink white wine. With shirtsleeves rolled up, bare elbows on the fake cold marble, I consider the twists and turns in my mind and in the shimmering marble. Then all at once, mingling with the glints on the counter and the whirlwinds in my head, she appears and she struts before me as if she were innocent. She takes her black hair that she's had cut off, that I used to love, and flings it in my face. My loved one, my sly one, says "sure, sure, sure," just like that, three times, then runs onto the street and doesn't come back. Setting off on the trail of the ungrateful son we made together one night in Spain at the hour when gardens collapse under their heavy scents.

Suddenly gusts of jasmine and orange blossom sweep into the smoke-filled room where I drain my glass. I'm astonished, for a long time, especially since I'm apparently the only one of the drinkers seated here to detect the sweet perfumes quickly transformed into the most acid vinegar, then all at once I fall asleep with my head on my arms, like a dead beast.

Miguel Almevida

Faster, always faster, I must live without wasting one minute, I've got just enough time, too many minutes wasted in the day, waiting for evening and the enchanted night that speeds along so quickly it's already over by the time I get my breath back. At eight p.m. I start getting ready and I take a long look at my face in the little mirror hanging on the bedroom wall. Behind me, my mother grows impatient and demands her share of the mirror. She doesn't like my face with makeup on and wants to obliterate it, replacing it with her own beautiful countenance. Fraternal struggle for a little piece of mirror. False eyelashes and mascara. Complicity and mutual adoration. This happens on those evenings when my father isn't home, when he's in the suburbs or the provinces, nails and hammers, going about his construction worker's business, and we're free, my mother and I, to go to the Paradis Perdu.

I offer roses to the customers there. I go between the tables selling roses. Tight trousers and silk shirt, hair falling onto my forehead and neck, I earn my living at the Paradis Perdu. No more school.

Every night, Jean-Ephrem de la Tour gives my mother a pass for the promenade gallery. She loves being there among the damp bodies crowded around her, she watches the show so intensely that it hurts her eyes, as if she were looking too long at the sun. Sometimes the warmth of a hand brushes her too closely, slips onto her, settles on her hip, burns her, makes her limp as a melting candle. She frees herself gently, smoothes the pleats of her black taffeta skirt and says: "Hands off."

Very quickly, she turns back to the show, all trembling and wet.

The greatest marvel of the evening is unquestionably Jean-Ephrem de la Tour, with plumes on his head and his quivering wings unfurled. He moves and dances. His tall body vibrates and sways. He is radiant; a thousand stars at once, all the way to the back of the house, pierce my heart, while I prick my fingers on the roses' thorns.

No echo lingers in the deserted auditorium. It's all over. Backstage, calm is gradually restored.

He is quiet, rested, after the shower water has gushed over his exhausted body. It seems to me that he's thinner. What had to happen is happening right now. Jean-Ephrem de la Tour invites me to his place. With my father at home and my mother keeping him company, I'm as free as the dark air of the nights, where I so love being just now.

Rose-Alba Almevida

After the festivities at the Paradis Perdu there is the conjugal vigil in the lodge on rue Cochin. Bare-chested, Pedro Almevida, my husband, is lifting weights. He won't fight with me until his biceps are just right.

He puts his shirt back on and sits astride a chair, facing me. He lists his grievances in a monotonous voice. He leaves nothing out and I get bored listening to him, I'm like an accused person waiting to hear the expected sentence. What's different now is that I don't. love him any more and he doesn't love me. The Paradis Perdu has come between us, like a continent of perverse wonders where I am happy and where he will never set foot.

"My wife is a thief!"

And he mentions the vacation money that I took to buy myself a dress from Marie-Christine a thousand years ago.

"My wife is a bad mother!"

And he talks about Miguel who is turning out badly and who sells roses at the music hall.

"My wife is a slut!"

And he keeps harping on about my mane of hair that was sacrificed to offend him.

"My wife is a whore!"

And he says that he knows all about it, about the promenade gallery and the Paradis Perdu.

"You aren't my wife any more and I'm not your husband."

And he takes me so forcibly that I bleed like I did the first time.

Jean-Ephrem de la Tour

It's engraved in Gothic letters on my performer's card. It's written in capital letters on the program of the Paradis Perdu. Jean-Ephrem de la Tour, star dancer. It would be unwise for anyone to try to trace all the names and surnames that have been lost along the way, as far back as the early records of the children's aid department.

Miguel Almevida. Little brother, oh, little brother of the poor. Not yet born. Not puny. Slim in the extreme. With great empty eyes and curls falling onto his forehead.

He's at my place. Advancing cautiously, leaving trails behind him on the thick carpet, like someone strolling along the soft sand of a beach.

Little by little he sees everything. His eyes veined with yellow and green fill with the strangeness of the place. Small gilt chairs, walls hung with crimson velvet, shelves of leather-bound books, concert grand piano, deep sofas, Chinese screen, huge mirrors waiting only for the slightest smile, the most secret tear in the shadow of eyelashes.

He thinks it surpasses the Paradis Perdu itself in magnificence. He is no longer moving at all. He's like an acrobat stopped short on his wire, in great danger of death. He looks at the brass barre on the wall, the pouffes on the floor, the subdued lamplight, the low tables covered with strange objects of gold and silver.

I extend the tour a little farther. I take him to see the first bedroom, the whirlpool bath that fills it completely, the second bedroom with the huge bed sitting on a platform, the white muslin canopy that falls like a bridal veil.

He listens and looks. He sits on the floor as if he'd fallen there. Frozen in place, knees pulled up to his chin, arms hugging his knees. The look in his eyes is that of a freshly killed hare.

Knowing perfectly well that he's had more than enough, I continue nonetheless to show him around my loft.

"Take a good look, Little Beast, look very closely at this wonderful loft that is mine, learn to call it by that strange name you've never heard before. Repeat it after me: loft, loft, loft. It's awesome, as you might say. You can see Paris by night through the big windows streaming with rain. Here, come closer. Take a good look. Lean out a little. It's no small matter, the seventh floor. Careful, don't get dizzy. It's shiny and shimmery down there on the pavement, from the rain. All those cars are heading somewhere, that's certain, each person with an idea in his head, an appointment, verifiable or fictitious, wipers beating against the windshield like a heart through tears. Watch out, you're liable to skid behind the Sacré-Coeur that stands there like a huge white cake. Twisted cars. Ambulances, police and firemen, screaming sirens. Soon we'll have to take stock of the night that is ending and decide between the dead and the living, while dawn falls over the city like the silver drizzle of rain."

I offer him champagne. In a barely audible voice, he asks for a Coke.

I tell him that his mother is very beautiful but that it won't last. "Once she's old, you'll have to throw her away and stop clinging to her like a sickly child." I laugh so hard I can barely hear what he says.

He protests with all his might, though he's already doubting the truth of his own words. "My mother will always be beautiful, she'll never be old, she'll always be beautiful. And as for me, I don't cling to anything or anybody." He's on his feet and looks like a lost child in a train station. He says that he wants to go.

"All right, Little Beast, go. It's raining and you'll get soaked. It's your choice if you want a scolding from your mother before daybreak."

His quick steps in the direction of the door. A little farther and he'll be outside.

I hold him back. Show him the full-length portrait painted by a perverse artist. "Take a good look at that portrait. It's me, with my feathers unfolded, nailed to the wall by my wings, like an owl on the door of a barn. Take a good look at my face at the moment of my ruin. It's the face I show sometimes to anyone who can bear it. Take advantage of it. My moment of truth won't return for a long time."

Suddenly he throws himself at me like a furious cat. He pounds my chest with punches that reverberate in my ribs. I smell his scent, the odour of a frightened and furious beast. I free myself and breathe deeply. My fatigue is immeasurable. I tell him to leave. He gets his breath back and delivers a sentence that doesn't seem to belong to him.

"I don't want you to be alive, or dead either. I would like you to not exist."

Miguel Almevida walks away down the deserted street, in the rain. No doubt he's afraid of the darkness and the emptiness around him, above all afraid of me. But until the end of the world he won't be able to stop himself from doing what he has to do in order to be afraid.

Miguel Almevida

I run in the rain. My shoes are full of water. My hair drips onto my neck. Loft, loft, loft — a strange word in my mouth, like a soft caramel that's been chewed and chewed again. Just one word, one small word that I've learned tonight and that means everything: the gilt chairs, the velvet walls. Jean-Ephrem de la Tour in his loft, like a Negro king in his castle all red and black. His noxious heart rendered visible on his entire ravaged body. The painter who did that is cursed, that's certain.

I run away. I go home, all alone in the exhausting night. I live in a rat hole, according to my mother. I sleep on a folding bed, right on the floor. I know the linoleum by heart, seeing it from so close, with its green leaves, its pink flowers, its worn spots, and its slightest cracks. But before I sleep I must appear before my parents.

Now the day is coming from every part of the city at once, grey and hazy. It pierces me more than the night itself, it wraps me in anguish from head to toe.

Rose-Alba Almevida

The garbage fire in the cellar. The firemen who arrive as I throw the first bucket of water onto the flames of the foul-smelling mound. A rat, two rats break away from it. I wish I could die. To die from having let the garbage accumulate, to die from not being allowed to let it pile up without being immediately punished by fire like a witch at the stake. To die of disgust, quite simply. It's as good as cancer or a heart that gives out. Killing me. My white hands, my scented body. I couldn't care less about the filth that this building secretes every day, like stinking crap.

In chorus, tenants and owners squawk at my door. "Madame Almevida! Madame Almevida! There's a fire! Do something!"

I'd like to throw the lot of them into a common grave to rot in silence, in the darkness of the earth, until their bones are stripped clean.

All day I have time only to sew, hunched over my machine which fills the house with its deafening racket. Driving me crazy. I work for thieves who exploit seamstresses working from home. It might last and then again it might not. One day I'll denounce them. For the time being, I need the money. I want a fur coat and I'll have it. I'll wear it to the Paradis Perdu. That's where I'm happiest, among creatures from a dream, adorned to the hilt, flung into the furnace alive, to the sound of thunderous music.

The promenade delights me more than anything else in the world. Its friendly darkness, its animal warmth against my hip, its delightful crowd of mature and knowledgeable men lying in wait in the shadows.

"Madame Almevida! Madame Almevida! You're dreaming! For heaven's sake wake up! The place is full of smoke. I'm suffocating. My eyes are burning. Do something!"

"Fire's under control. The firemen are sure. Go home."

Pedro Almevida, my husband, gently shoos them out of the lodge, shoves them almost tenderly, leads them to the stairs in the dark, flicks the switch. Five a.m. in November. They aren't a pretty sight in the bright light, the tenants and owners together. You old pile of brightly coloured bathrobes, I don't like you, I never have and I never will. I'll go to the Paradis Perdu and take a break from all of you and from life in general.

At last we're alone. I take off my pink satin dressing gown. Before I get into bed, I accuse my husband of throwing his cigarette onto the garbage in the cellar. He shrugs, says I'm crazy. I think he's laughing in my face. I look for my son. I find him asleep, as usual, on his little camp bed between the buffet and the table. I'll never know when he came home. Too much bedlam tonight to know what's really going on in my house.

Miguel Almevida

Quiet nights in the fifth arrondissement. My father left the house right after he tried to strangle my mother. She was probably screaming too loudly before she blacked out, and he was afraid of annoying the owners and tenants, who would agree to call the police.

He lit a cigarette and left, smoking — for Spain, he said. Taking none of the necessary things, no jacket, no pants, no razor, no shirt, no clean underwear, no baggage, nothing, hands in his pockets, cigarette stuck in his mouth, red-faced though, like someone who's not in his normal state. His heart was beating so hard you could hear it in the kitchen until he left through the front door.

Sitting on the floor, half-choked, my mother came back to life, with the marks of my father's fingers around her neck.

"All he had to do was not look under the bed where I hide my things. All he had to do was not see my fur coat in its golden cardboard box. But who could have told him about Monsieur Athanase?" my mother finally managed to say, between two fits of choking.

The coat lies on the floor, sprawled like a great dead animal.

Rose-Alba Almevida, half-undressed and torn apart and trembling, drags herself over to the coat, strokes it gently as if she were petting a cat. "This coat cost me a lot." Then come some incoherent words interrupted by sobs, about the promenade gallery and the encounters that take place. "He told me I was as lovely as a picture and he took me to the furrier right after we left the four-star *hôtel de passe* on the quay."

Something terrible went on inside my father's head, as if the red cape that's waved before a bull had been waved right in front of my father's narrow brain, as if thin banderillas had been planted in his heart, and my father came very close to murdering my mother, the short breath of murder up against my father's furious face. He couldn't tolerate that, the thought of murder. He went away, taking nothing. Maybe he's hoping to find what he wants back in Spain — their old life, intact and pure, my mother with her long black hair, smiling at him. Me, still unborn. Her, innocent of me and of him. Content to wear her bridal crown perfectly straight on her raven hair arranged in an extravagant chignon. Her long veil falling to the floor in cascades of transparent white. If only the blond prostitute who's taken my mother's place on rue Cochin in Paris would disappear forever. What my father couldn't do I'll do myself one day. The murder of Rose-Alba Almevida will take place. I, the son, cover my face with my hands and weep. Dishonour is upon our house, posted at the entrance like a quarantine notice. Already contaminated by dishonour here in my rat's hole, I love my mother more than anything in the world. I forgive her for everything.

Rose-Alba Almevida

The marks on my throat are changing colour, from red to violet, from violet to blue, from blue to a dirty yellowish green. I wrap a silk scarf around my neck. I hide my wound and my fury behind the silk that was given to me by the man from the promenade gallery. I'm hibernating in my lodge. I'll stay there as long as that cruel necklace, a gift from Pedro Almevida, my husband, stays around my neck.

My son looks at me with eyes filled with alarm. He puts ice cubes in a transparent plastic bag around my neck. He speaks softly so as not to rouse the last scene, still alive, lurking in the four corners of the darkened kitchen. I can't tolerate any light. Or the lodge, open to everyone. I've pulled the curtain over the glass door that opens onto the landing. A few calls for help come to me, I'm lethargic, they fall around my bed like blunt darts.

"Stairs not done for days, polish, polish, I'm expecting a delivery, stairs caked with dirt, Lafayette, Lafayette, delivery, delivery, urgent, urgent . . ."

I hear distinctly the voice of the blond student with the rough moustache who shouts: "Marquise, come out! We want you on the stairs lively and affable, as usual!" He repeats: "On the stairs!

The stairs, Marquise!" His loud laugh rings out from the bottom of the stairwell to the top.

I plug my ears, I close my eyes, I imagine diamonds and gold, fine pearls and blue sapphires to hide my wound, heavy necklaces that sparkle around my neck like a hundred flaming suns when I open my lynx coat partway. And I fall asleep. Sleep and dreams intermingled. My son takes advantage of my sleep to fly away to the Paradis Perdu. I shall join him there when I'm healed.

Money has no odour, they say. But I can smell it as soon as it's inside the house, in the blue box under the bed, its odour as pungent as strong Spanish tobacco, reassuring and comforting. And now I can sense the absence of money, it's like breathing emptiness, a trough in the air that I fall into. Vertigo. My husband's pay has disappeared along with him. Alone with my son. My sewing machine takes off like a galloping horse. "It will kill you, my girl," my mother would say. "The entire marriage bed is yours, my darling," my father would say, "stretch out there full length, full width, like a cat in the sun." Thus encouraged by my father, I fall asleep so calmly that the entire earth, with its gnashing, its trials and tribulations and its terrors, turns against my ear and I can't hear it breathing its warm oppressive breath. The crazy planet that I live on. The blessed promenade where I collapse.

Jean-Ephrem de la Tour

"Your mother's a whore, Little Beast, your mother's a whore. It was to be expected. I know everything. Monsieur Athanase told me everything. There's no reason to lose your head and drop me like an old sock. You son of a whore, you're never here when I need you. But here you are at last with your arms full of roses, your idiotic eyes showing just enough fear to please me. Where were you yesterday? And the day before? Do you mean to tell me you were taking care of Rose-Alba Almevida, as if she were a martyr under the absent gaze of God? She'll get over the conjugal marks on her magnificent neck, the neck of a Roman matron. And did I have to be on my own twice, without you, facing a ferocious audience on gala evenings? I didn't lift my leg high enough, got a cramp in my right thigh, lost the beat. Tremendous panic all through my body. Beak open, wings folded. Flap, flap, flap. Without you in the front row I break down. I go to pieces. I melt under the lights like a candle on an altar. Little Beast, I like to see you, to be seen by you, when I dance. I want you there, paying attention, holding on to your seat, marvelling at me, endlessly. Nothing else exists, including your mother. I like you to torment yourself over me."

Miguel Almevida

He insulted my mother. He called her the most terrible name that you can possibly call a woman.

I shouted: "And what about you? What about you? Did you never have a mother?"

"Never!" he replied, his great laugh revealing his white teeth, stretching his cheeks to his ears. "Never! Never!" he said again forcefully.

It calmed me a little to know that he's never known a mother and it helped me understand the insult that's always on the tip of his tongue, all ready to say, as soon as a conversation turns to mothers in general. And then, very quickly, my indignation slipped through my fingers like sand and I knew that he had good reason to complain about me.

He speaks more and more softly, at the very edge of dream and waking. About shortened breath, about gleaming black skin gone dull all at once, about shame and disaster, about my unforgivable absence.

I think that in his unhappiness, he luxuriates in sad words in order to dazzle me with sadness and to make me a prisoner of my bedazzlement like a blind owl flung into the light.

Is it possible that one day I'll be totally blind and a prisoner of Jean-Ephrem de la Tour? For the time being, I just have to promise that I'll always be there when he does his act.

I draped his big towel over his shoulders and led him, dripping sweat and still elated from his own lamentations, to the shower. Before he disappeared under the rushing water, he said in a powerful voice:

"Tell your mother that Monsieur Athanase will be waiting for her at the promenade as soon as she's recovered from her husband's insults."

He emerges from the shower, streaming wet from head to toe. I bring him a dry towel, big and wide, roughly textured the way he likes it. I get ready to rub him down like a horse after a gallop. Very gradually I'm getting used to his black nakedness.

Rose-Alba Almevida

No more being waited on hand and foot, no more bandages around my neck, no more contrite manner or indignant heart. I'm convalescing. I'm visibly regaining my strength. I long to go back to the Paradis Perdu. I return to the promenade gallery where Monsieur Athanase is waiting for me. The man who wrung my neck will pay what he must. Once, only once with Monsieur Athanase, such a beautiful lynx coat as a bonus, but it isn't enough for my hunger and my thirst, my anger and my indignation. There will be a long series of encounters with Monsieur Athanase. In a four-star hotel. Along the Seine.

In the darkness of the room, Monsieur Athanase prefers no light at all, I could swear that the *bateaux-mouches* enter the dark air here, brushing against me like seaweed as they pass by in the night. He puffs like an ox long before I spread my legs. He's crazy about me. I'm crazy about what he does to me, what he teaches me to do. We'll go to hell, the two of us. Together or separately. It doesn't matter. In any case, Monsieur Athanase won't be forever. He's too hairy and he smells of cologne.

The true demon in this world is Jean-Ephrem de la Tour.

Monsieur Athanase is going to America. He gave me a gold ring with a small blue stone that sparkles with a thousand fires. It reassures him about my faithfulness during his absence and it dispels his fears about the true generosity of his pathetic little soul. I wear my ring on the fourth finger of my left hand, like a bride. I ask forgiveness of no one, not God, not Pedro Almevida, my husband.

When Monsieur Athanase returns from America, if he returns, I'll tell him about the apartment I dream of, bright and vast, with an unobstructed view of the Eiffel Tower.

Miguel Almevida

He looks at me as if he were turning me over and over in his fingers. His gaze on me, prying and incorruptible. He adds up my virtues and my flaws: "Back too bent, rib cage too narrow, legs magnificent, legs of a girl, with no hair or knobby kneecaps."

I tell him I've always wanted to be a girl and that I was persecuted on account of it.

He replies: "You would not seek me out had you not already found me. It was Christ who said that, along with some other incomparable things. Remember, for one brief moment in your mother's belly you were both boy and girl, before the preposterous choice to be only a boy. Remember how good it was, remember how sweet it was, a tiny girl without fingers or feet, a teeming mass of cells, the tiny sex of a girl, sealed like an envelope."

I can't understand what he's saying and I think I'm crying. He gets a dress for me from his big closet, a gorgeous dress that's just my size, and high boots that fit me perfectly, and elegant lingerie, everything makes me so happy I could die. He has just bought it all for me. I undress right away. My boy's clothes fall to the floor around me. Briefly, he sees me naked.

For a long time I study myself in the mirror that covers one whole wall in the bedroom of Jean-Ephrem de la Tour. What I see surprises me, but I also recognize my true reflection in the mirror, haughty and innocent. I smile tenderly and my image replies, tender and smiling too, the image, the image, the beautiful image of me, Miguel Almevida.

He pulls me away from my contemplation, takes me out of my reflection in the mirror in a way, forces me to be real, to stand opposite him in the middle of the room, sharp and alive, changed into a girl and proud of it.

He offers me champagne. I learn how to drink, while my nose prickles and my eyes fill with tears. He talks to me about my hair, which is like silk, increasingly long and silky.

"Little Beast, thou art Little Beast and upon this Little Beast shall I build my happiness."

He laughs hysterically with delight. He pulls himself up abruptly, comes over to me and strokes my hair for a long time, absentmindedly, no doubt meditating in silence upon his imminent fierceness.

Jean-Ephrem de la Tour is entertaining visitors. I serve champagne and, with a lock of hair over one eye, act as his maid in my brandnew dress.

With their backpacks, leather jackets, and worn jeans I barely recognize the performers from the Paradis Perdu, without makeup or fake jewels, just as they are, pale and dishevelled.

Jean-Ephrem de la Tour says that he's never let down either a lady or a gentleman. He laughs. He struts. He's vulgar. A lout. He selects a pale redheaded girl for himself and takes her into the bedroom with the canopy bed. He asks me not to leave, to be his witness, to wait there against the bedroom door until everything is done and well done between the redheaded girl and him.

I race away as if there were a mob at my heels. My heart sickened. My gorgeous dress wet with tears.

Rose-Alba Almevida

I dream about a little gilt chair with a red velvet seat, a little gilt chair just for me, Rosa, Rosie, Rosita Almevida. When I'm sitting on my shining chair, the frills of my skirt spilling over on all sides, I shall dominate the entire world and no one will be able to bring me down from my pedestal. When I dream like that it sometimes happens that I go beyond the permitted limits of dreaming, that I see too much, in mass and in number, that I imagine a whole string of little gilt chairs standing against the flaking walls of my hovel, like so many gleaming nuggets. I am enthroned in gold and red velvet. It's my beloved son in whom I've placed all my indulgences who is urging me towards these extremes of daydreaming. Has he not described for me ecstatically, repeatedly, the splendours of Jean-Ephrem de la Tour's loft?

I must see it all with my own eyes — the furniture and the silver cutlery, the books bound in tawny leather, the carpet, curly like a bison, the pure gold and the crimson velvet, the immense bed and its white gauze, false candour and light mist. One night will no doubt be sufficient for me to know everything about the black angel of the Paradis Perdu, all his secrets save for the mystery that exists between him and my son. I tremble because

Jean-Ephrem de la Tour is black with green hair and I am white with hair dyed yellow like wheat. I tremble because my son adores that man who torments him, in the way that flagellants adore God during Holy Week processions in Seville.

He came home very late last night, half-suffocated in the muffled dawn, his tears running onto his neck, his girl's dress all crumpled, his girl's legs visible below his girl's dress. Barely wakened from a heavy sleep, I saw it all in a fog. My son with his overlong hair, his heartbreaking tears because of a redheaded girl, he said. And I, I knew that it was because of Jean-Ephrem de la Tour. I hated that man, my son's torturer, and, at the same time, I wanted to sleep with him so as to go deeper into humiliation and be ruined along with my son.

Now that Monsieur Athanase isn't there, I'm terribly bored at the promenade. The men who brush against me in the shadows hardly deserve to live. More than ever I want Jean-Ephrem de la Tour to be crucified by his wings, then dropped onto the stage like a great black butterfly, his wings beating. The orchestra will play a shuddering tune then and I shall hear it from far beneath the earth when I'm nothing but ashes and dust.

Tonight, there's no performance at the Paradis Perdu. My son is sleeping like a sick child. I'll go to Jean-Ephrem de la Tour's place. I'll surprise him at home. I'll soak up the overly sweet air of his loft. I'll inhale American cigarettes, black skin, the deep carpet, the huge bed, the books dressed in fragrant leather. I'll be like a retriever with an extremely keen nose who is let loose in public. Perhaps I'll learn where Jean-Ephrem de la Tour keeps all that money he throws out his windows. I'll bask in red velvet and white muslin. I'll sleep with that very black man in a canopy bed. And maybe in return he'll give me the little gilt chair with the red velvet seat that I dream of.

Miguel Almevida

Her flowered muslin dress brushes against me as she goes by. Her agitated breath passes over my narrow camp bed on the floor in the kitchen where I pretend I'm asleep. Exasperating, the scent of sun-soaked geranium lingers in the room after she's shut the front door behind her. I listen to the dwindling sound of her footsteps on the sidewalk. I get up and dress. Knowing nothing about my mother's rendezvous. Wanting more than anything in the world to know nothing about what she's doing so late in the dark. I convince myself that Monsieur Athanase is back from America. Very quickly I stop thinking about my mother and abandon her to her fate, the fate of a fallen woman on the run in the night. Only one thing is necessary. To get that well and truly into my head. To reconcile with Jean-Ephrem de la Tour who offended me greatly with a passing girl, redheaded and pale as a sparrow's egg.

Once I'm outside, the familiar streets move along beneath my feet, like conveyor belts in the blue-grey of the night, illuminated here and there by the yellow glow of streetlamps. Rue Cochin, rue de Pontoise, boulevard Saint-Germain. Place Maubert. The black entrance to the Métro. To dive into it. The long journey to the end of night. Departures and arrivals. The wait on the deserted platforms. The open air. The Butte. Its hills and staircases. Sit at a café terrace. Wait for the time to pass, let it slip by in the distance without me. To be in this deserted café as if I weren't there. Go over the things that are vague in my heart. Drink coffee, one after another.

Now they're bringing in the tables and chairs. Obliged to get up and leave. Fear every footstep that brings me closer to Jean-Ephrem de la Tour. It's the first time. Me, all alone in the night, going to him though he doesn't expect me. Repeat his name like a prayer, Jean-Ephrem, Jean-Ephrem, stretch his false surname like a long thread of melted cheese that grows longer, de la Tour, de la Tour . . . Laugh at his theatrical nobility. Forgive him for the red-haired girl. Adore him like a god who is devastating and cruel. Hell and paradise for a child with nothing better to do.

I have the key. I go inside as if I were at home. Everything is in order. The red walls, the heavy curtains, the closed piano. You can almost hear the air in the room as it moves slowly, in rhythm with a calm invisible breathing, without even a hint of mist on the big mirror. Nothing is happening here. The ardent nocturnal life is some-where else. Imagine that absent life. Feel it as it gradually makes its way into my heart like a foreign woman of whom one must be wary. Look at the two closed doors in the red wall. Desire more than anything in the world that these doors stay closed forever. Want to wall them in with stones, like tombs.

It won't be long now. The air is thick all around me. I must learn the things I'll need to know for all eternity. I've looked at the wall in front of me so hard it finally opens, so slowly that I die by inches.

My mother is a fury. Her muslin dress swollen with anger, Rose-Alba Almevida, more radiant than the crimson walls, a flame glowing red, walks out of the room that has the canopy bed, straightens her puffed sleeves, passes by without seeing me, slams the door, and goes out onto the street.

He follows behind her, towering, lanky, says that he's impotent and that it's my fault. "You're never here when I need you, you little piece of trash."

I answer him so softly that no one but me can hear what I say, so softly I am at the very edge of absolute silence. "I'm going to kill myself."

Letter from Jean-Ephrem de la Tour to Miguel Almevida

My child, my sister, Little Beast, little spouse whom I see in my dream, little piece of flotsam destined for the fire of heaven, tiny lost thing. I must bid you adieu. Note carefully, by the way, that strange word "adieu." I've obviously read too many books that are beyond me. Remembered whatever words aren't ordinary. Adieu, then. I must tend to my affairs. For a long time I played an angel in the theatre and a beast in bed, with fleeting companions. I've been kicked out of the Paradis Perdu. Now I must swallow the unbreathable air of this world, without thinking about it, and slip away. Towards other climes. Enigmas don't have such a hard life. Soon you'll know everything.

But where shall I send this letter? Needless to say, not in care of your mother, that beautiful victim. I'll look for you everywhere. You'll never know it most likely. I'm writing just for myself. No stamp or postman. I'll look for you in the streets. I'll keep the secret of you to myself, like a hidden treasure.

Without breaking any silence, I am yours,
Jean-Ephrem de la Tour

Miguel Almevida

Which of them, my mother or Jean-Ephrem, having betrayed me equally, pushes me gently towards the Seine?

I lean over as far as I can to smell the bland odour of the water.

Behind the grey clouds the day is slowly breaking. On the riverbank, a clochard lies on his cardboard, rolled up in his blanket, yells at the top of his lungs in his dreams, shouting that it will be a beautiful day.

From looking so hard at the slow and monotonous Seine, I grow weary and listen to the booming, rusty voice of the clochard who proclaims the beauty of the day and calls to me in secret.

In no time I dash up to the Quai de la Tournelle and shake myself like a dog coming out of the water.

The day is dawning on all sides at once. I must flee without further delay. One last stop at the lodge to get my things. One last look at my sleeping mother. Her party dress in a heap on the chair. She who offered herself and was refused is sleeping like a baby gorged with milk. And I, her offended son, am leaving her at this moment forever.

Soon the silence of the sleeping house will be broken. Footsteps everywhere, on the stairs, the landings, doors opening and closing, voices greeting or grumbling. Hurry, before it's too late. Hurry. The unlivable time in which I exist is becoming thinner, like worn fabric. So tired. My legs give way under me. To leave my mother without further delay. The keys there, hanging on the wall! Madame Guillou's key, cold and shiny between my fingers. Madame Guillou on vacation in the south. Take advantage of her empty apartment. I enter her place like a thief. Go directly to the bedroom. Collapse on the bed on my stomach, my face in the pillow. Risk choking because of the tears. Fall asleep in Madame Guillou's bed.

Madame Guillou

They should all be kicked out. Loathsome people. The father, the mother, the son. Drive them out of the house without delay. The father, on the run who knows where, the mother, in desperate straits screaming from door to door, "Have you seen my son, Miguel?" and he, he, the little hypocrite who stayed in my apartment while I was away, he, the child I once loved, the serpent that I warmed in my bosom. Found his list when I came home from my vacation, sitting prominently next to the telephone on my night table where he'd forgotten it. It said:

Before leaving:
- *buy package of Lustigru egg noodles and just leave half*
- *put a quarter litre of water in Evian bottle*
- *close all shutters*
- *tune radio back to France Musique*
- *buy Fruit d'or sunflower oil margarine*

The perfect crime. All traces wiped clean. Now he is sinking deeper into the savage night as though nothing were amiss and no one the wiser. That child ate and drank in my house, he slept in my sheets. If I ever catch him. He, he, the affectionate little youngster I used to love.

Rose-Alba Almevida

A voice can be heard in the fifth arrondissement, an endless moaning and wailing, it is Rose-Alba Almevida, weeping for her son who has disappeared, refusing consolation because he's been gone for five days now.

"God of my childhood, give me back my son and I'll become a virgin again forever, beneath the habit and the veil as you want me to be, for eternity, amid the lighted altar candles, the swaying sanctuary lamps, the chubby-faced cherubs and rapturous madonnas."

At the same time, there are the outcries of Madame Guillou who's come back from her vacation. Wrinkles in her sheets, a strange odour in her bed, too much order throughout the apartment. And particularly that list left next to the telephone, written by Miguel Almevida, that she sticks under my nose.

Madame Guillou repeats "forcible entry," "breach of trust." Her upper lip curls up over her little green teeth, as if she were about to nip with a poisonous bite.

And I, I, his mother, the first to be betrayed, the first to be trampled on, I am foaming with rage. Light has been shed on every mystery. My son is a runaway, my son is a squatter, my son is a hoodlum. I'm going back to the Paradis Perdu. That will teach the child that I brought into this world for my damnation and his.

Miguel Almevida

On the run from my mother's, can't go back to Madame Guillou's, no fixed address, I've been wandering from street to street since this morning. Windbreaker creased, shirt soiled, shoes worn down, I drag my muddy soles. As inattentive as in school, mind blank, ravenous, I am going I know not where to lose myself once and for all. And nothing more need be said.

The grey street, the grey sidewalk, the white stripes at intersections, the rotten gutter, the red lights, the green lights. I know only what I need to know about the city in order to advance, step by step.

For a while now garish lights have been reflected on the street. I walk through puddles of colour — red, green, blue, yellow. The air thickens, filled with obscene invitations from the clubs lined along the sidewalk. Voices come to me, muffled and hoarse. Pleasure is offered to me from door to door by barkers in richly coloured uniforms.

Who then has brought me here? Dragging me by the hand, pushing me by the shoulders, bringing me to this place where I'd sworn I would never return?

The scent of the wet air reminds me of the scent of his big body streaming under the shower.

If I don't watch out, Jean-Ephrem de la Tour's massive apartment building will rise before me like a blind fortress against the black sky.

My footsteps, without resonance or echo, resemble those of cats lost in the night.

No, no, I didn't want that.

Jean-Ephrem de la Tour

One tiny lamp, at the end of a long cord, stands in the middle of the room. All that is left of the light is there on the floor and I'm on the floor as well, looking as if I'm using a campfire for light. All around me, the carpet like a wasteland. Here and there, spots left bare and brown where the furniture has been taken away.

All the treasures that were here have been removed — furniture, books, trinkets. Even my bed, covered with white muslin. The life that I lived here, flashy and mad, has been carried off and taken far away. I expect that I'll be taken too.

Movers came with a truck. They left a void around me. Now I'm sitting cross-legged in the middle of my devastated loft. I'm eating a ham sandwich and picking up the crumbs as they fall to the carpet.

My big body, kicked out of the Paradis Perdu for obscure reasons, scrutinizes itself in the low muted glimmer. My hands on my knees look dead, one beside the other. My face frozen like a stone. My bare feet displaying the calluses of the skilled dancer. I persist in this implacable examination. I pretend to look over my badly lit body for a trace of some unknown sin that might be the cause of everything.

No defeat then. Real life is quite simply elsewhere. Instead of real life I'll have a look at what it's like elsewhere. Plenty of boredom most likely, and disgust, which is worse than boredom. All of that before the arrival of soothing habit and recovered laughter.

The rain has left long spurts of scattered drops on the glass. I press my face against it but it doesn't cool me. On the other side of the world, the city in mist. Its damp breathing. I watch for the long car that's supposed to come for me at any moment.

From my position it's impossible to see the small silhouette hugging the walls, advancing along the sidewalk towards me, slow and light as a shadow.

Miguel Almevida

He is standing in the doorway looking furiously at me, as if I shouldn't exist before him.

"Where have you come from at this hour of the night, Little Beast?"

I look at him too, at this man who, dead or alive, was made to be seen by the greatest number of people on stage in a theatre.

People emerge from the elevator, scatter on the landing, and laugh very loudly. Hurriedly, Jean-Ephrem de la Tour shows me into his loft.

A single lamp, standing on the floor, throws light onto the black carpet. There are no other lamps anywhere. Jean-Ephrem de la Tour's loft no longer glows, vast and deep as far as the eye can see. Every corner now is full of darkness. So empty as to discourage you from living. Our enormous shadows on the wall no longer look like anyone. Is it here that everything will end? We don't know what to do with our eyes, mouths, ears, with our hands that hang down on either side of our bodies. It's a question of knowing who will be the first to break the silence. He, the embodiment of my ruin? Me, so overjoyed by him that it could kill me? Now each of us facing the other, each in his skin as in a fragile shelter.

It is he who moves first. He paces the room, barefoot, holding his shoes, then throwing them violently at the brass barre left behind on the wall.

He turns back to me. "I don't have much time. You'll have to leave in a hurry."

He sits back down on the floor and puts on his shoes, slowly, like a child tying laces for the first time.

He talks so softly that it's like a breath, just barely perceptible against my ear. "I'm expecting someone."

It doesn't surprise me that he is expecting someone, nervous as he is. If it's my mother I'll kill him, and my mother too. I'll be handcuffed and taken to court. I enunciate clearly, as if I had a part in a play and weren't fully there: "I hope it isn't my mother."

He laughs and he says that it's not. He takes his shoes off again and starts doing exercises at the barre. It reminds me of the Paradis Perdu and I want to cry. He puts his shoes back on and looks out the window. He talks with his back to me, still looking out the window.

He seems to be speaking to someone invisible, someone floating between heaven and earth, right there at the level of the seventh floor. Jean-Ephrem de la Tour's breath leaves condensation on the streaming wet window.

"I've been confiscated. Do you know what that means, confiscated? They took away everything that was here. The furniture and knickknacks. Even the gold chain from my neck and the bracelet from my wrist."

I wish I could console Jean-Ephrem de la Tour, take him out of his unhappiness. I murmur, just in case, as if I know what I'm talking about: "Didn't you pay your rent?"

That makes him laugh and he turns towards me, animated and happy as if he were going to start dancing again. "I like you, Little Beast, you make me laugh. But I don't have much time left to look after you just now. Didn't pay my rent, as you say. Didn't pay. Anything. Debts everywhere. A mob is after me. I have to go away."

"Take me with you." I say this as if the words had escaped from me by themselves, without my wanting, without my even opening my mouth, a little like blood on the surface of the skin, barely touched by the air as it passes.

"Little Beast, you're dreaming. And me, I was made for living, for living without reins and without scruples, do you understand?" His dazzling teeth so close to my face, his breath on my cheek. His gaze fixed in a strange squint, like a wolf's.

I look at him as long as I can, wanting desperately never to lose sight of him. I tell him he looks like his portrait and that it drives me to despair.

He turns away. He stands at the window again. The bad weather exasperates him. He complains about the fog and the height of the building not letting him see what's going on in the street. Says again that they're waiting for him and that he ought to go down right away. He unplugs the little lamp on the floor and tucks it under his arm to take away. "It's all I have left. Better bring it along."

I hear him breathing in the dark as my heart fills the room with rapid, muffled beating. His shadow against my shadow in the dark room.

Jean-Ephrem de la Tour

Nothing to say. Nothing to explain. Keep my distance. Let him mind his own business. Let me mind my own. Tell him again to go away while a vague glimmer enters the room through the open window. I believe he's shivering in the mist that sweeps in here as if we were at the seaside. I'd rather he insult me and cry openly. At one stroke I'd be rid of the patient and furious expectation of my punishment.

I hear his voice that's come from I know not where, across the grey and empty room: "I would so much have liked to be a girl and to marry you."

I talk to him about a wedding gown, white and billowy and falling to the floor. I tell him that his love of clothes will spell his ruin. I recite to him the hallowed formula of marriage. I insist on the bride's obligation to share everything with her husband, for better and for worse, till death do them part.

He answers so quietly that I guess rather than hear what he says. "Yes, yes, I want all that, I want to marry you."

Night lies slack over all the city. And yet it grows brighter and brighter in this empty room where I'm shut away with Miguel Almevida. From looking in the dark so much I'm able to see as if it were daylight. A little while longer and I'll have his dazed face before me, staring at me. That must be avoided at all costs. Talk in the darkness of my lowered eyelids. Give in to theatrical lines worthy of the Paradis Perdu. Admit that I'm going on a trip to the sun and the sea, in the company of a very mature and very rich lady. Then move on in sheer fantasy.

"As for my pitiful heart, which is as old as a hundred-year-old Chinese egg, I leave it to you as a token. Do what you want with it. All my sins are there. I have only one thing in mind at present, to start life again as if nothing had happened. Go, Little Beast. Go, I beg you, go."

For another moment he stands there before me, ready to flee, motionless and mute, while the blood inside him rushes and stirs as if for a sudden death.

I tell him again to go. "Go now, Little Beast. Go. They're waiting for me."

He has the misfortune of being unable to leave. I push him towards the door. I bid him adieu, tenderly, like in a novel.

Miguel Almevida

Not at my mother's or at Madame Guillou's or at Jean-Ephrem de la Tour's. There's no place where I can sleep and eat, laugh or cry, in peace. Driven away from everywhere. I go down onto the deserted riverbank. Day is breaking in the grey sky. There's no clochard to declare that the day will be beautiful.

I am heavy, so heavy, like a woman carrying a child on her back. Jean-Ephrem de la Tour, my husband. I shall deliver him from his evil. I shall take responsibility for his burden, fasten it to me like a big stone to drown me.

After looking for a long time at the Seine lapping at my feet, I begin to see images half-dreamed in the shuddering water. The Spain of my parents, with its white houses, its silvery olive trees, its green vines all in a row, undone by the invasive water when I bend over it. Someone sacred I don't yet know is preparing a suit of light for me, in secret, in the midst of the waves and grey ripples, for when I'll have arrived among the dead.

Madame Guillou

Those people are impossible. The son has drowned himself in the Seine, the mother is screaming so loudly you can hear her in the street; as for the father, rumour has it that he prowls the city in the hope of getting his wife back and erasing all dishonour from his house.

Translator's Afterword

A translator is above all a reader, a close and careful reader: she reads a work — in this case a novel — again and again, probing its deepest secrets, attempting to comprehend and reinterpret the author's chosen images and words. I have performed this labour of love on six novels by Anne Hébert, and now on this, her final one. While a translator's interpretation of a text will necessarily determine its form in the new language, the author's way of looking at and interpreting the world of her fiction will mark the translator, too. Anne Hébert has changed forever the way in which I view and interpret aspects of certain landscapes, landscapes both natural and emotional. Above all, she has left me, she has left all her readers, with a vision of a world in which, despite prevailing darkness, the ultimate victor is light.

— Sheila Fischman